For Gary, Harry, and Larry

Library of Congress Cataloging-in-Publication Data
Tanen, Sloane.
Coco all year round / by Sloane Tanen ; photography by Stefan Hagen.—1st U.S. ed.
p.   cm.
Summary: Coco the chicken finds something special about each month of the year.
ISBN-10: 1-58234-709-3 • ISBN-13: 978-1-58234-709-7
[1. Months—Fiction. 2. Year—Fiction. 3. Chickens—Fiction. 4. Stories in rhyme.] I. Hagen, Stefan, ill. II. Title.
PZ8.3.T14517Coc 2006   [E]—dc22   2006000959

First U.S. Edition 2006
Printed in Singapore
Designed by Teresa Dikun
1 3 5 7 9 10 8 6 4 2

Bloomsbury Publishing, Children's Books, U.S.A., 175 Fifth Avenue, New York, NY 10010

COCO ALL YEAR ROUND

by Sloane Tanen
with photography by STEFAN HAGEN

BLOOMSBURY
CHILDREN'S
BOOKS

JANUARY

January isn't easy.
It's cold and wet and often breezy.

But New Year's Day there is no school
So I can ice skate on the pool.

FEBRUARY

I wanted to make something special for Ray
To show him I care on Saint Valentine's Day.

I think he was pleased
with the heart that I painted.
His mom was so dazzled, she actually fainted.

MARCH

On Saint Patrick's we march in the yearly parade.
There's music and dancing and green lemonade.

I walk down the street with my whole Girl Scout troop.
It would have been fun, had I not slipped in poop.

APRIL

I think my favorite day at school
Is April First—it's April Fools!

My teacher doesn't have a hunch
We're hiding something in her lunch.

MAY

The greatest month of all is May.
Why? Because it's my birthday.

Presents, parties, all my friends—
I hope that this month never ends.

JUNE

In June we all go to the sea.
I bury Dad, he buries me.

I'd like nothing more than to bury my mother
If she weren't so busy burying my brother.

JULY

Magic camp is in July.
My friend Dashell makes cards fly.

While Sammy learns to float on cue,
I slice Hank Carter clean in two.

AUGUST

Splashland would be much more fun
Than driving to Aunt's in the hot summer sun.

My brother's annoying, the car smells like feet;
The air is so sticky, I'm stuck to the seat.

SEPTEMBER

September is here; we're all back in school.
Today's Show and Tell, and I brought Raoul.

Though I would have preferred a cat I could carry,
My brother's allergic to everything hairy.

OCTOBER

A devil, an angel, a princess, a queen?
Guess what I am this Halloween!
I planned my own costume and glued up this suit . . .
But PLEASE pass out candy—no one likes fruit.

NOVEMBER

There's lots to eat on Thanksgiving Day:
Stuffing, green beans, yam soufflé.
And even though it's sort of quirky,
We don't believe in eating turkey.

DECEMBER

The holiday season is filled with surprise—
The hat I made Grandma brought tears to her eyes.

And here's an idea I'm just now believing:
I *almost* like giving as much as receiving.